D0190462

ADVENTURES
— AT —
HOUND HOTEL

PICTURE WINDOW BOOKS
A Capstone Imprint

Adventures at Hound Hotel is published by Picture Window Books,
a Capstone imprint
1710 Roe Crest Drive
North Mankato, Minnesota 56003
www.mycapstone.com

Library of Congress Cataloging-in-Publication Data
Names: Sateren, Shelley Swanson, author. | Melmon, Deborah, illustrator.
Sateren, Shelley Swanson. Adventures at Hound Hotel.
Title: Stinky Stanley / by Shelley Swanson Sateren ; [illustrated by Deborah Melmon].
Description: North Mankato, Minnesota : Picture Window Books, an imprint of Capstone
Press, [2017] | Series: Adventures at Hound Hotel | Summary: Alfie Wolfe's dislike of
baths, and his habit of wearing shoes without socks, has resulted in a case of stinky
feet—but they may be just the thing to keep Stanley, a Labrador retriever with a
fondness for dead fish, from trying to run away from the Hound Hotel.
Identifiers: LCCN 2016012617| ISBN 9781515802211 (library binding) |
ISBN 9781515802235 (paperback) | ISBN 9781515802259 (ebook (pdf))
Subjects: LCSH: Labrador retriever—Juvenile fiction. | Dogs—Juvenile fiction. |
Odors—Juvenile fiction. | Kennels—Juvenile fiction. | Twins—Juvenile fiction. |
Brothers and sisters—Juvenile fiction. | CYAC: Labrador retriever—Fiction. | Dogs—
Fiction. | Odors—Fiction. | Kennels—Fiction. | Twins—Fiction. | Brothers and
sisters—Fiction.
Classification: LCC PZ7.S249155 St 2017 | DDC 813.54—dc23
LC record available at http://lccn.loc.gov/2016012617

Designer: Heidi Thompson

Printed in the United States   4022

Stinky Stanley

by Shelley Swanson Sateren
illustrated by Deborah Melmon

TABLE OF CONTENTS

CHAPTER 1
That Totally Stinks. 9

CHAPTER 2
Trapped by Ms. Snoot. 18

CHAPTER 3
Squashed Flat as a Frisbee. 26

CHAPTER 4
You Rude Boy. 34

CHAPTER 5
Dog of Steel. 42

CHAPTER 6
Something Smells Fishy. 50

CHAPTER 7
Close to Fainting for Real. 55

CHAPTER 8
Happy-Dog Dance. 60

ADVENTURES
AT
HOUND HOTEL

IT'S TIME FOR YOUR ADVENTURE AT HOUND HOTEL!

At Hound Hotel, dogs are given the royal treatment. We are a top-notch boarding kennel. When your dog stays with us, we will follow your feeding schedule, give them walks, and tuck them in at night.

We are always just a short walk away from the dogs — the kennels are located in a heated building at the end of our driveway. Every dog has his or her own pen, with a bed, blanket, and water dish.

Rest assured . . . a stay at the Hound Hotel is like a vacation for your dog. We have a large play yard, plenty of toys, and pool time in the summer. Your dog will love playing with the other guests.

HOUND HOTEL
WHO'S WHO

WINIFRED WOLFE
Hound Hotel is run by Winifred Wolfe, a lifelong dog lover. Winifred loves dogs of all sorts. She wants to spend time with every breed. When she's not taking care of the canines, she writes books about — you guessed it — dogs.

ALFIE AND ALFREEDA WOLFE
Winifred's young twins help out as much as they can. Whether your dog needs gentle attention or extra playtime, Alfreeda and Alfie provide special services you can't find anywhere else. Your dog will never get bored with these two on the job.

WOLFGANG WOLFE
Winifred's husband pitches in at the hotel whenever he can, but he spends much of his time traveling to study wolf packs. Wolfgang is a real wolf lover — he even named his children after pack leaders, the alpha wolves. Every wolf pack has two alpha wolves: a male one and a female one, just like the Wolfe family twins.

Next time your family goes on vacation, bring your dog to Hound Hotel.

Your pooch is sure to have a howling good time!

CHAPTER 1
That Totally Stinks

I'm Alfie Wolfe, and there's one thing I hate: baths.

Almost every night my mom says, "For Pete's sake, Alfie, please go take a bath. Wash those stinky feet with soap before I faint from the smell!"

Problem is, Mom always says it right when I'm doing really important stuff. Stuff like handing out bedtime treats to the dogs in our dog hotel.

Most of the time, I avoid the bathtub without Mom noticing.

But this story isn't about my stinky feet. Well, not totally. It's about a stinky dog named Stanley. A Labrador retriever, to be exact. A yellow Lab, to be exacter.

Stanley loved to roll in dead stuff, like fish. The deader the better.

In my opinion that wasn't a problem. But this was: When he stayed at Hound Hotel, his owner, Ms. Snoot, wouldn't let him play outside. *All* dogs should play outside. It totally stank. I never felt sorrier for a dog.

Stanley showed up at Hound Hotel one morning last month. It was the peak of summer and super hot.

Before Stanley arrived, my twin sister, Alfreeda, and I were sitting on the kitchen floor, eating our cereal. That's totally normal at our house.

See, our mom was writing another book about dogs. As usual, the kitchen table and chairs were covered with her writing stuff. She sat at the table and typed on her computer.

Alfreeda and I wolfed our cereal out of dog bowls. (Don't worry; we *did* use spoons.) That's normal at our house too. All the regular bowls were dirty and piled in the sink.

We own more dog bowls than regular bowls. Why? Because there's really only one part of the store our mom likes to shop in — the dog department.

Alfreeda read a Hound Hotel new-visitor form while she ate. I read over her shoulder. It was information about Stanley, written by his owner, Ms. Snoot:

My dearest Hound Hotel workers,

Like a true Labrador retriever, my sweet boy, Stanley, loves to play catch with sticks, balls, and Frisbees. Also like a true Lab, he runs very fast. It gives him great joy to tear around outside.

He would stay outdoors all day long, if I allowed it. But I don't allow it, now that it's August. He gets much too hot, dirty, and sweaty. I simply cannot stand a stinky dog.

Therefore, I expect you to keep Stanley inside his pen while I'm gone. He may go outside for short bathroom breaks, but no running around!

I expect my dear Stanley to smell as sweet as a rose when I return from my overnight trip. Thank you.

Sniffingly yours,

Ms. Snoot

Alfreeda finished reading and said, "What? Stanley can't play outside at all?"

"He'll be bored out of his mind," I cried. "That totally stinks!"

"Hmm?" Mom said. "Alfie, did you say something stinks?"

She looked away from her computer and sniffed the air. "Something really does smell horrible in here," she said. "What *is* it?"

She stood up and wandered around the kitchen. First she sniffed the pile of dirty dishes in the sink.

Then she sniffed the full trash can.

She opened the refrigerator and sniffed in there too.

She closed the refrigerator and sighed. "Bad smells everywhere," she said. "This place needs a good cleaning. But I just can't do it right now. I have a book deadline and a hotel full of dogs to care for. And your dad's gone again."

Our dad was gone for two weeks this time. He was on another wolf-study trip up north.

"But where is that *horrible* smell coming from?" Mom asked. She walked around the room, sniffing in corners.

Suddenly Alfreeda cried, "Found it! Gross!" She held my shoes by her fingertips. Then, quick as a flash, she threw open the back door and tossed my shoes outside. She shivered. "Eww, those stunk. Bad. I can't believe I touched them."

"Alfie," Mom said in a firm voice. "You *have* to start wearing socks with shoes. And you *have* to do a better job of washing your feet with soap."

"Okay,"
I muttered.

Mom sat at the computer again. About two seconds later, she sniffed. "I still smell it," she said.

"I smell it too," Alfreeda said.

Mom stood up and marched toward me.

"Sit, Alfie," she ordered.

I sat.

"Lift, Alfie," she said.

I lifted my foot. I knew the drill. Mom had me trained like a prize-winning show dog when it came to feet-smelling time.

Mom sniffed my toes and slapped her hand over her nose.

"Alfie!" she cried through her fingers. "For Pete's sake! Did you take a bath last night? Did you even *touch* the soap? Your feet have never smelled worse. They smell as bad as . . . as . . . dead fish!"

My face got hot. I didn't say anything.

Alfreeda covered her nose too. "Can't you smell yourself?" she asked me.

"I don't know," I muttered. "My nose is a long way from my toes."

"Upstairs, Alfie. Now," Mom said. "Take a bath. Wash those feet — *with soap.*"

"But, Mom, Stanley will be here soon!" I cried. "I have to talk to Ms. Snoot. I have to make her let Stanley play outside. He'll be crazy bored if he's stuck in his pen!"

"Alfie," Mom said in her I-mean-business voice. "You may *not* come inside the kennel building with awful-smelling feet. There can't be one bad smell in Hound Hotel. Customers will think it isn't a healthy place for their dogs. Our house may not always smell the best. But the hotel must be clean and smell fresh. Understand?"

"I guess so," I muttered.

With that I spun around on my stinky toes and tore upstairs. I'd take a bath at record speed. And somehow, I'd find a way to talk some sense into Ms. Snoot.

Hang tight, Stanley Old Boy, I thought. *Alfie will save the day.*

CHAPTER 2
Trapped by Ms. Snoot

I leaped up the stairs two at a time. I turned the bathtub water on full blast.

Right away, the bathroom got steamy. While I waited for the tub to fill, I drew a dog on the fogged-up mirror. A Labrador retriever, to be exact. A Lab with a Frisbee in his mouth, to be exacter.

Then I drew a wolf. That reminded me to practice my wolf howls.

I always practice my howling skills in the bathroom (when I am supposed to be taking baths). My howls sound extra loud in there.

I'm not bragging, but practice has made me Alpha Howler around our place. ("Alpha" means "first" or "top.") See, whenever my dad is home, he and I have howl-offs. We use a timer to see who can howl the longest. We use a recorder to see who can howl the loudest.

I always win.

Anyway, the morning Stanley arrived, I howled super loud. Like an alpha wolf calling his pack over a wide, foggy valley.

I turned off the tap and started to take off my T-shirt. Right then the hallway clock barked. It went *WOOF* eight times.

Eight o'clock? I thought. *Already?* Stanley was supposed to arrive at eight!

I threw open the window and leaned out. I looked at the kennel building at the end of our long driveway. That's where the Hound Hotel office is and where the dog pens are.

A big, fancy black car was parked by the office door. Ms. Snoot's, I figured. I had to get down there quickly.

I tugged my shirt back on and ran downstairs. I flew outside and grabbed my shoes off the driveway. *No time to put them on,* I thought, as I sped to the kennel building.

Running must've kicked my brain into gear. I got a great idea. Suddenly I knew how to talk Ms. Snoot into letting Stanley play outside. I'd give her a tour of Hound Hotel's great play yard! Yes, sir, I'd show her the huge, grassy, fenced-in area full of super-fun dog toys.

Ms. Snoot would take one look at it and say, "Oh, my! Stanley simply *must* play in this lovely doggie yard. For hours and hours! Think of all the *fun* he'll have!"

Seconds later I was standing beside Mom's desk in the hotel office. I panted like a bulldog on a steamy hot day. It *was* hot outside, and the short run had made me sweat all over.

Alfreeda crawled around the office floor super fast, chasing after Stanley. He ran around the room, sniffing everything: plants, chairs, the trash can . . .

In fact, Stanley stuck his nose deep in the can and tipped it right over. Trash spilled on the floor. He dived at an old brown apple core and started to chew it.

"Yuck, Stanley. Not a good snack," Alfreeda said. She dug it out of his mouth and led him away from the trash. She held him tightly around the neck. She got him to sit, but he wiggled like crazy, trying to get away.

Ms. Snoot didn't even notice. She sat in a chair beside Mom's desk. Her long, pointy nose pointed straight at Mom.

Mom studied Stanley's new-visitor form. Then she cleared her throat and said, "Of course, we always obey our customers' wishes. But honestly, I'd be happy to give Stanley a bath tomorrow morning before you return. Then he could play outside and really enjoy his stay here. We like our guests to get a lot of exercise. And the dogs love the play yard —"

"Excuse me, Mrs. Wolfe," Ms. Snoot interrupted. She raised her long, pointy nose in the air and sniffed. Her face wrinkled. "I'm sorry," she said in a weak voice, "but . . . but what on earth is that awful smell? It smells like . . . like . . . *dead fish!*"

Mom's mouth fell open as wide as a largemouth bass's mouth. Her eyes popped out until she looked like a blowfish. She looked at me, then at Ms. Snoot, then at me again.

"Alfie," Mom said under her breath. "Go outside. *Right now.*"

Well, believe me, I tried. I spun around to leave, but I couldn't get past Ms. Snoot. She'd stood up and had started to sway back and forth on her high heels.

"Terrible smells make me faint," she said in a weaker voice. "Oh dear, I'm going to pass out."

I tried to duck around her left side. She leaned that way and blocked my path.

I tried to dart around her right side. She swayed that way.

Then she leaned her bony arm on my shoulder and laid her head on top of my head. Man, I'm telling you, Ms. Snoot STANK — like rose perfume!

The perfume smelled strong and terrible. I would've fainted, if I were the fainting type.

Actually, I'd smelled that perfume before. My mom has the same kind. She wears it on date nights with Dad. It's horrible.

Suddenly Ms. Snoot passed right out. She tipped over and squashed me to the floor. Her pointy nose landed right beside my stinky toes.

"Ms. Snoot!" Mom cried, rushing to help her customer.

"Ouch!" I shouted. "Her bones are as sharp as thorns! And she stinks like a rose bush full of huge wild roses. Gross! Get her off of me!"

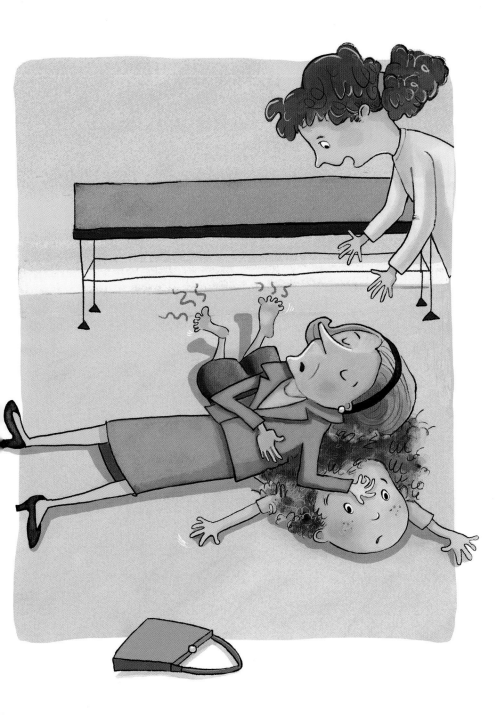

CHAPTER 3
Squashed Flat as a Frisbee

"Alfie, *shh*," Mom said. "How rude!"

"Ms. Snoot didn't hear me," I said. "She's passed out. She's super bony and stinky, Mom. Get her off of me!"

That's when Stanley broke free from Alfreeda. He ran across the office and jumped on top of Ms. Snoot. He lay right over her, like she was a dog bed.

Now TWO bodies squashed me almost as flat as a Frisbee. Ms. Snoot's bony legs and arms dug deeper into me. Seriously, OUCH!

Then Stanley started to lick my feet.

"Stop that," I laughed. "It tickles!"

But Stanley didn't stop. He licked super fast and tickled my toes like crazy.

"Mom, help!" I cried. "I'm getting poked all over by a stinky, thorny rose bush. And it's like a cow is covering my feet with spit —"

"Alfie, SHH!" Mom cried. "Stop being rude!"

"But Mom, fainted people can't hear," I said.

"Okay, okay. Just a minute. Calm down, Alfie," Mom said.

Together, she and Alfreeda dragged Stanley off Ms. Snoot and away from my feet. Then Alfreeda tugged Stanley down the hallway toward the kennel room. That's the big room full of dog pens at the back of the building.

The other dogs started to bark. A few terriers, a couple beagles, and an old wolfhound had stayed overnight. They all yipped or howled, saying a super-loud HEY in dog talk to Stanley.

He barked like crazy right back at them.

Mom rolled Ms. Snoot off me. Slowly, Ms. Snoot came to. "What happened?" she asked in a weak voice.

"Please hold that thought, Ms. Snoot," Mom said. She turned to me and whispered, "Go outside, Alfie. Take your stinky shoes with you."

"My pleasure," I said, jumping up.

I raced out of the office and around the side of the building. I peeked in an office window. Mom was handing Ms. Snoot a cup of water.

"Dear me," Ms. Snoot said, rubbing her forehead. "Where on earth am I?"

"You're at the Hound Hotel," Mom said. "The best dog-boarding kennel this side of Lake Dee-Oh-Gee. Ms. Snoot, your Stanley is in very good hands here. We treat our dog guests like family, like our own dear children.

"I promise you," Mom went on, "we *will* keep Stanley in his pen while you're gone. The twins will play all kinds of fun games with him inside. He'll have a wonderful time. So! You'll return from your trip tomorrow morning?"

"I guess so," Ms. Snoot said weakly.

She stood up and walked toward the door on shaky legs. Then she headed toward her car in a zigzaggy line and zoomed away.

About half a second later, Mom darted outside and found my hiding place. She put her hands on her hips and frowned.

"Alfie Wolfgang Wolfe," she said.

Well, I know I'm in the doghouse when my parents say my full name. "In the doghouse" means in BIG trouble.

"Your stinky feet almost cost me a customer," she said. "Enough! Go take a bath.

Now! With soap! Don't come back until you smell as sweet as . . . as . . . a *rose*!"

"Yuck," I muttered. But I sure didn't say any more. I was in enough trouble already.

I dragged my stinky feet toward the house.

"Find some other shoes to wear too," Mom called. "Sandals, boots, anything. Don't wear that awful pair again until I've had time to double-wash them. And wear socks!"

"O-KAY," I called back.

I dragged my stinky feet indoors and upstairs to the stupid bathroom. I stuck my stinky big toe in the tub water. Cold. Yes, sir, the water had turned cold by then. Even though it was a steamy hot day.

Yep, my warm, happy morning had turned cold and gloomy. Now I didn't even feel like practicing my howling skills anymore.

This is the boringest morning in Hound Hotel history, I thought. *For Stanley* and *me. I've got to find a way for us to have a good time.*

I sighed and started to take off my T-shirt.

Just then Alfreeda yelled, "Alfie!"

Her voice came from outside. I ran to the window and leaned out. Alfreeda stood below, waving her arms in the air.

"Come help!" she cried. "Quick!"

"Help with what?" I called.

"Stanley!" she cried. "Somehow he got away from me and pushed open the play-yard door. Then he ran across the yard and jumped over the chain-link fence!"

"Wow," I said. "That's a super-high fence!"

"I know!" she said. "He's running toward the woods, toward Lake Dee-Oh-Gee. Mom says you have to come down here and help us catch him. Hurry! Run!"

"Okay!" I ran downstairs in two seconds flat and tugged on my stinky old shoes.

Sorry, Mom, I thought. *No time to find a different pair. Or a pair of socks.*

I had a runaway dog to catch!

CHAPTER 4
You Rude Boy

I tore down the driveway, chasing after my sister and mom. Mom was in the lead. She'd already made it to the end of the long, winding path through the meadow. She was about to disappear into the woods.

I ran past our chicken coop and apple trees. Then I blasted past my sister. Usually she's the alpha kid in the running department, but I outran her this time.

I ran through the meadow and seconds later entered the dark woods. It was a little cooler in there, but not much. I raced down the worn path, around trees and big rocks. I leaped over tangled roots and thick-growing green stuff.

"Stanley!" I kept calling. "Where are you, boy? Come here, boy!"

About a minute later, I came out into blinding sunshine. The air was hot and thick and hard to breathe. I wiped my forehead and wiggled my toes. My shoes felt like a couple of mini bathtubs full of steamy hot sweat.

Standing in the hot sand didn't help. Heat shot through my shoes and up my legs.

I looked down the long shoreline of Lake Dee-Oh-Gee and spotted Mom. She stood with her hands on her hips, shaking her head. She was watching Stanley. And smiling.

Suddenly Alfreeda leaped to my side. She dropped to the sand, puffing and panting like an overheated pug.

"I HATE days this hot," she said.

"Hey, kids! Look!" Mom called. "Stanley must've smelled this dead fish from the play yard! There's a strong south wind today!"

"Gross," Alfreeda said. "He's rolling in it!"

"Looks like fun," I said.

Stanley lay on his back in the sand, feet in the air. He rolled over the dead fish, back and forth, about 20 times.

Then he jumped up and rubbed his nose in it.

After that, he did a happy-dog dance on top of it.

Finally Mom said, "Come on, boy. That's enough. We need to get you cleaned up."

She pulled Stanley by the leash toward the edge of the woods. Before they even reached us, I smelled the stinky guy. My nose filled with the horrible smell of dead fish. Long-dead fish that had been lying in the hot sun.

"Yuck." I swallowed hard to keep from throwing up. Alfreeda and I both pressed our nose holes shut. The smell was so bad, we darted ahead of Mom and Stinky Stanley.

I kept looking back to check on Mom. Stanley sure didn't want to leave the lake. He tugged hard on the leash and kept trying to turn back.

"Kids," Mom called, "run ahead and fill the washtub half full with warm water. When I get there, I'll need your help lifting this big, strong guy into it."

Alfreeda and I raced to the kennels. Just as we got the water running, Mom's cell phone barked. (Our phones don't ring, they bark.)

"I'll get it," I said, running to the office. I answered Mom's phone the way she'd taught us. She had Alfreeda and me trained like show dogs in the telephone skills department.

"Hello, this is Hound Hotel, the perfect country-vacation place for your dog," I said in my clearest, cheerful-est voice. "Alfie Wolfe speaking. How may I help you?"

"You rude boy!" barked a woman.

I held the phone away from my ear and stared at it. *What?* I thought. *I didn't say anything rude.*

I put my ear back to the phone and said, "Um . . . excuse me? Maybe you have the wrong number?"

"I most certainly do not," the woman barked. "This is Ms. Snoot. Let me speak to your mother."

Uh-oh. Not Ms. Snoot!

"I'm sorry," I said, "but she's out of the hotel at the moment. She's . . . um . . . walking a dog. May I take a message?"

"Yes, you may, you rude boy!" she snapped. "Tell your mother I'm turning back. Tell her I've decided not to take my overnight trip after all.

"Tell her," Ms. Snoot barked on, "that I simply cannot leave my dear Stanley in an unclean kennel. All those germs! Frightful! He might get sick! You tell her that I will be there in ten short minutes to pick him up — never to return!"

"But Ms. Snoot," I said. "Hound Hotel is spotless! My mom keeps it crazy clean. There aren't any germs in the whole place. Look, I'll be honest about what was so stinky, okay? It was actually my . . ."

Oh man, I thought. *How can I tell a customer that my feet smell like dead fish?*

Ms. Snoot didn't say anything. That's when I realized she'd hung up.

I dropped the phone on the desk and raced to the meadow. Mom was tugging Stanley toward the kennel building.

"Mom, hurry!" I cried. "We've only got ten minutes to get Stanley smelling great. He's got to smell as sweet as . . . as . . . a *ROSE*!"

CHAPTER 5
Dog of Steel

Stinky Stanley sure didn't want to come into the kennel room. He slid on his rear end and dug his claws into the floor.

A powerful stink filled the room. The other dogs started to bark like crazy.

"Cool it," I told the crowd. "Nobody's getting a fish snack. It'll smell fresh and clean in here again real soon. Stanley just needs a bath, that's all."

Well, the second I said the B word, Stanley howled. He yanked the leash backward, toward the door. Then he started spinning in circles.

The leash tugged Mom forward. She almost fell flat on her face. Stanley got all twisted in the leash.

"Hold on! You're going to be just fine, Stanley," Mom said. She untwisted him and pulled him gentle-like toward the washtub.

That was Stanley's cue to play dead. He rolled over and lay flat on his back. He didn't move a single muscle. He even closed his eyes.

He looked deader than a dead fish (because fish can't close their eyeballs).

I leaned over him and opened his left eyelid. "Hey, pal. Nice try, but you can't fool me. I know you're alive and kicking. Don't take it personal, man, but you really stink. Way worse than my feet. I'm almost throwing up, standing this close to you," I said.

"Listen," I went on. "We'll give you a real fast and . . . uh . . . real *fun* b-a-t-h, okay?"

I hated lying to a dog about a bath being fun. But now we only had about eight minutes left!

I turned to Alfreeda. "Look, if we don't get Stanley smelling like a rose, Ms. Snoot will never bring him back here. I like him, even if he stinks. I want him to keep coming back."

"Me too," Alfreeda agreed. "Let's do this."

She grabbed Stanley's left paw. I grabbed his right. Then we started to drag the big guy toward the washtub.

He was super heavy, like a boat full of dead, smelly fish.

Mom helped by pushing his rear end.

It took lots of strength, but we finally reached the tub.

"Yikes," Alfreeda said, looking at the poodle clock. "Only five minutes left!"

"Okay," I said. "On the count of three, lift. One . . . two . . . THREE!"

With a lot of groaning, we lifted Stanley over the edge of the tub and lowered him toward the water.

"Almost there," I said.

Suddenly Stanley stuck his legs straight out, real stiff. His paws grabbed the rim of the tub, two on each side.

His leg bones locked into place. Now his body was a bridge over the water. A hairy, super-straight bridge that didn't sag one bit in the middle.

"Whoa, Stanley's got super-strong legs," Alfreeda said.

"Like steel," I said. "I wonder how long he can hold that position."

Well, Dog-of-Steel Stanley kept right on holding on. And on. And on.

"Wow, this has to be a record," Alfreeda said.

"No kidding." I patted Stanley real understanding-like on his stinky back. "Come on, bud," I said. "Just get in the water. You really do need a bath."

Stanley howled again. Loud.

"Stop saying b-a-t-h, Alfie," Alfreeda said.

"Sorry!" I said. "So should we force him in the water or what?"

"No," Mom said. "Something must've made him afraid of b-a-t-h-s. We definitely don't want to force him."

"But most Labs love to swim," Alfreeda said.

"True," Mom said. "Give him another minute. He'll get tired and plop in. I'm going to the storeroom to get the extra-strength dog shampoo. Be right back."

The poodle clock tick-ticked away. I was getting pretty nervous. Stanley's legs didn't even shake.

About half a minute later, Mom came back with a bottle of shampoo.

"Does it smell like roses?" I asked.

"It's unscented," she said. "That's best for a dog's skin."

"But it *has* to smell like a rose," I said. "That's Ms. Snoot's favorite."

A-ha! Of course! I snapped my fingers. "Your rose perfume, Mom," I said. "The junk you wear on date nights with Dad. I'll go get it. You guys give Stanley a speedy bath. Then I'll spray him."

"Great idea," Mom said.

I dashed out of the kennel building, up our driveway, and into the house. I leaped up the stairs three at a time, then ran to the dresser in my parents' bedroom. I said hi to Dad's picture and grabbed the little bottle of perfume.

In two seconds flat, I was back outside in the bright sunshine. Just in time to see a car pull up.

Oh no, I thought. *Ms. Snoot's here!*

She killed the engine and opened the car door.

I flew right past her. I didn't say hi.

I didn't offer to help her out of the car.

I didn't even offer to help her up the steps to the office door.

Nope.

And yep, I was acting totally rude, but I had work to do. I had exactly thirty seconds to spray Stinky Stanley all over with rose perfume. Bath or no bath!

CHAPTER 6
Something Smells Fishy

I blasted past Ms. Snoot, into the office, across the room . . . and tripped right over a rug. The stupid chew-bone-shaped rug in the middle of the stupid floor.

"Yikes!" I yelled.

I shot forward and crash-landed on my stomach. OOMPH! The wind got knocked right out of me. The glass bottle got knocked out of my hand too. It bounced on the wood floor but didn't break. It shot across the floor and slid under a low shelf.

That second the doorbell rang. It sounds like a crazy terrier barking at a mail carrier. *YIP! YIP! YIP!* You can hear it all over the kennel building. All the dogs started barking super loud.

The doorbell must've made Stanley leap off the washtub too. He came tearing down the hallway toward the office.

"Come back, Stanley!" Alfreeda cried. "You didn't even get your paws wet!"

Stanley charged into the office and jumped on me. OOMPH! The wind got knocked out of me again.

That's when Ms. Snoot opened the door and stepped inside. Stanley did an excited *rrr-OOOF*, leaped off me, and jumped on her. She teetered on her high heels and flopped into a chair.

"What on earth is that horrible smell?" she cried, covering her pointy nose.

She wasn't kidding. The room stank like a hot beach covered with long-dead fish.

"Let me explain —" Mom began.

"Don't bother, Mrs. Wolfe," Ms. Snoot snapped. "I'm afraid I *must* tell my friends about your terribly unclean dog hotel. I daresay, none of them will ever bring their dogs here."

Mom's mouth fell open in total shock. She couldn't even speak.

I jumped up and put my hands on my hips, mom-style. "Listen here, Ms. Snoot," I said. "No one keeps a cleaner kennel than my mom!"

"Quiet, you rude boy," Ms. Snoot snapped.

Mom looked even more shocked.

"He didn't say anything rude," Alfreeda said.

"My sister is right, Ms. Snoot," I said. "Why do you keep calling me rude?"

"Because you called my bones *thorny*," she said. "You called my rose perfume *stinky*."

"Wait a second," I said. "We thought you were out cold when I said those things. You were just *pretending* to faint? Something smells kind of fishy about the way you're acting, Ms. Snoot. Like maybe you're not telling the whole truth about something. Maybe you should come clean about it."

"Alfie!" Mom said. "*Shh!*"

Ms. Snoot frowned at me. She stood up fast and marched toward the door.

"Come, Stanley," she ordered. "We're leaving!"

Suddenly I remembered something Mom had taught us twins: The customer is always right, no matter what.

I could *not* let Ms. Snoot leave all angry-like. I could *not* be the reason for losing a single Hound Hotel customer — even a rude one.

"Wait!" I said. "I'm sorry, Ms. Snoot. I take back what I said. You're totally right, about everything. How can we make our service better for you?"

CHAPTER 7
Close to Fainting for Real

Ms. Snoot stopped. Her long, pointy nose was one inch from the door. She spun around and stared at me.

My heart beat fast. *Uh-oh*, I thought. *I totally ticked her off now.*

"What did you say?" she asked.

"I . . . um," I stammered. "I said I was sorry. No matter what, I shouldn't have said that stuff."

Ms. Snoot looked down at the floor and sighed. She started to chew on her bottom lip. "I see," she said.

Stanley sat on her feet and whined.

"Well, I *do* need to come clean," Ms. Snoot said at last.

"Huh?" I said. Now I was completely bewildered. Come clean about what?

"The thing is," Ms. Snoot explained, "Stanley used to stay at Wagging Tails Inn on the other side of Lake Dee-Oh-Gee. He always ran away to roll in dead fish. He's not allowed to stay there anymore. That's why we're here. And that's the true reason I wanted you to keep him inside a pen. So he wouldn't run away."

"I'm afraid he already has," Mom said.

Ms. Snoot shook her head at Stanley. "Bad dog!" she said. She looked at Mom and muttered, "I'm so sorry. To you *and* your son. For lying and for behaving rudely. Please forgive me."

"That's quite all right," Mom said.

"I just don't know what to do about my stinky Stanley," Ms. Snoot said.

"He's not a bad dog," Alfreeda said. "He's just behaving like a true Labrador retriever, like his kin back in history. They were raised to fetch nets full of fish out of the Labrador Sea. That's how they got their name."

"Really?" said Ms. Snoot.

Usually my know-it-all sister bugged me. But right then I was glad she'd dumped that fact on Ms. Snoot. Stanley wasn't a bad dog. He was just acting natural.

"I guess nothing can keep my boy from running away," Ms. Snoot sighed. "I'll never be able to leave him here or at any dog hotel. Come, Stanley. We've caused these people enough trouble."

"Wait!" I said. "I've got an idea."

I tugged off my shoes.

"Alfie!" Mom cried. "What are you doing?"

"Gross!" said Alfreeda.

Now an odor as powerful as Stanley's dead fish filled the room. It smelled like TEN boats full of dead, smelly fish.

Stanley went *WOOF* and leaped straight at me. He stole one of my shoes, dropped to the floor, and started to chew it. He gnawed on it like he'd never tasted anything so tasty in his entire life.

Everyone covered their noses. Ms. Snoot looked close to fainting — for real.

"Sure, my idea stinks," I said. "Still, it's a great one. I'll explain."

"Hurry up, Alfie!" Alfreeda squeaked. "Before we all pass out!"

CHAPTER 8
Happy-Dog Dance

"I know how Stanley can hang out in the play yard and not run away," I said.

"Explain," said Mom.

"Please," said Ms. Snoot.

I could barely hear them. Their hands still covered their mouths and noses. The thick stink cloud hung around us.

"He doesn't have to be cooped up all day," I said. "I'll stay in the play yard with him. He won't run away again because my feet smell like dead fish. And we all know how much he *loves* the smell of dead fish. He can roll on my feet or chew my shoes — whenever he wants to. He'll forget all about Lake Dee-Oh-Gee. He'll get lots of exercise and have lots of fun."

"Interesting idea," Ms. Snoot said through her fingers. "I like it. Your smelly feet may be just what we need!"

"Let's give it a try," Mom said through hers.

"Yay!" I jumped high and spun in the air. "Come on, Stanley. Follow me. First we'll grab all the balls and Frisbees."

He barked and did a happy-dog dance.

"Then," I continued, "we're taking our stinky selves outside!"

So that's how I got to spend the whole hot day outside, playing with Stinky Stanley. We tore around so much, my feet got even dirtier and stinkier. Stanley got dirtier and stinkier too.

I always remembered to stand upwind, so Stanley would smell my feet instead of Lake Dee-Oh-Gee. He rolled on my toes a lot, like they were ten little dead fish.

We played catch for hours. When he got tired, I got him water to drink and let him rest. He'd lie down and chew my stinky shoes until he felt like tearing around again.

I'm proud to say he didn't try to jump the fence even once.

That afternoon, I thought, *Maybe it stinks that I'm keeping this great dog all to myself.*

"Hey! Want to play catch with us?" I asked my sister.

"No way," Alfreeda called from the play-yard door. "I'm not coming near you two."

Well, I asked.

So the day was perfect — with a capital P! After dinner (Mom made me eat outside), when the sun started to set, Mom cornered us two stinky guys.

"Okay," she said. "It's b-a-t-h time. For both of you."

"Aww, Mom —" I started.

But then I got another great idea. This one didn't stink at all.

I told Mom the idea, and she agreed.

Out in the play yard, I filled our old kiddie pool with water. I found floaty toys and beach balls. Mom brought out the dog shampoo, plus a bar of soap and some people shampoo.

And would you believe it? Good Old Stanley jumped right into the water! He let us cover him with shampoo bubbles and rub him clean. He even let me hose him down too.

After that he woofed at me eight times. I knew exactly what he meant: "If I can do it, you can too."

"All right," I sighed. I sat in the kiddie pool, in my swimsuit, and rubbed my feet with soap. I rubbed until they gleamed like fish scales.

"Better?" I asked.

Stanley barked.

I even did a good job of shampooing my hair for once. Mom and Alfreeda couldn't believe it. I couldn't believe it either. I kind of liked the way I smelled too.

The next morning, right before Ms. Snoot picked up Stanley, he still smelled pretty fresh and clean. But I wasn't taking any chances.

"Come here, boy," I said. I sprayed him with rose perfume.

He sneezed.

"I know it's gross," I said. "But the next time you come to visit, I'll have my great-smelling feet and shoes ready for you. Promise."

WOOF! WOOF! WOOF! he barked.

I knew just what he meant: "Can't wait, Alfie!"

Is a Labrador Retriever the Dog for You?

Hi! It's me, Alfreeda!

I bet you want your own smart, friendly, playful, loving Labrador retriever now too, right? Of course you do! Labs make great pets for families. I mean, most families. But before you zoom off to buy or adopt one, here are some important facts you should know:

Labs need lots of love and attention. They want their owners to spend a lot of time with them and play with them a ton. If Labs are left alone too long, they'll get bored and lonely. Then they'll bark too much and chew things they shouldn't. So if you're the kind of family that's always away at work or school or soccer games or music lessons, don't get a Lab (or any dog). Get a goldfish.

Labs are very active dogs. They need big spaces for playing and running. They're fast runners and need to tear around every day. A large fenced-in yard is great. If you don't have one, put your Lab on a long chain. Or take your Lab to a dog park often. If you don't have a big yard or a dog park nearby, don't get a Lab. Get a hamster.

Labs need to be brushed once a week. Brushing removes dead, matted hair and helps keep a Lab clean. If you're too busy to brush your Lab once a week, then you're too busy to own any animal. Get a pet rock instead.

Okay, signing off for now . . . until the next adventure at Hound Hotel!

Yours very factually,

Alfreeda Wolfe

VISIT
HOUND HOTEL
AGAIN WITH
THESE AWESOME
ADVENTURES!

Learn more about the people and pups of Hound Hotel

www.capstonekids.com

About the Author

Shelley Swanson Sateren grew up with five pet dogs — a beagle, a terrier mix, a terrier-poodle mix, a Weimaraner, and a German shorthaired pointer. As an adult, she adopted a lively West Highland white terrier named Max. Besides having written many children's books, Shelley has worked as a children's book editor and in a children's bookstore. She lives in Saint Paul, Minnesota, with her husband, and has two grown sons.

About the Illustrator

Deborah Melmon has worked as an illustrator for more than 25 years. After graduating from Academy of Art University in San Francisco, she started her career illustrating covers for the *Palo Alto Weekly* newspaper. Since then, she has produced artwork for more than 20 children's books. Her artwork can also be found on giftwrap, greeting cards, and fabric. Deborah lives in Menlo Park, California, and shares her studio with an energetic Airedale Terrier named Mack.